The Chatty Parrot

by June Woodman
Illustrated by Ken Mor...

GONDOLA

Parrot is always chatting.
She loves to talk and she
always says things twice.
Sometimes the other animals
wish she was not such
a chatterbox.
"Wake up! Wake up!"
she shouts at Lion just as
he wants to go to sleep.
"Go away, Parrot," yawns Lion.

"Don't forget! Don't forget!"
she squawks at Spider.
"Don't forget what?" asks
Spider, on his way out.
"Your shoes. Your shoes,"
says Parrot.
"I have all my shoes,"
says Spider, "but now
I forget where I was going."

"Watch out! Watch out!"
screeches Parrot at Alligator.
He is about to trip on a rock.
"Thank you, Parrot," says
Alligator. He turns and trips
over Elephant instead.
They both fall in the mud.
SPLAT. Elephant is very cross.
"That Parrot is too chatty,"
he grumbles.

One day Alligator runs to see
the other animals. Crash!
He trips over Elephant's foot.
"Have you heard?" he gasps.
"Parrot has lost her voice!"
"Hooray!" shout Lion, Spider
and Elephant together.
Kangaroo hops off to pick
some lemons for poor Parrot.

Monkey runs after her. There is a bee's nest at Kangaroo's place. He climbs up to the nest. Parrot can see him. She flaps her wings, but she cannot talk. The bees can see Monkey too. They get very cross when he dips his paws in their honey. The bees begin to buzz.

Monkey runs away, with honey dripping from his paws.
Parrot flies after him.
He runs past Lion's den.
Drops of honey fall on Lion's head, but he is asleep.
A long line of ants comes marching along, on the trail of the honey. They march up on to Lion's head.

Lion wakes with a roar.
The ants are all over him,
and they tickle!
Lion looks at Parrot.
"Why didn't you warn me?"
he roars. She can only flap
her wings. "Water! I must
jump into water!" roars Lion.
He rushes off. Parrot goes too.

Hippo is by her pool.
She is looking at herself
in the still water.
"I do look pretty today,"
she sighs. Suddenly Lion
roars up. The ants are
marching across his nose.
They make him go cross-eyed.

Lion dives for the pool.
He bumps into Hippo.
SPLASH!
They both fall in the water.
Hippo looks up and sees Parrot.
"Why didn't you warn me?"
she groans, but Parrot can
only flap her wings.
Now the water is overflowing!
It goes flooding down the hill.

Parrot goes after it.
At the bottom of the hill
is Giraffe's house. He is
mending the roof of his tall
shelter. He is always putting
his head through it.
Suddenly, he is up to his
knees in water.
"Why didn't you warn me?"
asks Giraffe. Parrot can
only flap her wings.

Giraffe runs away to escape from the flood. He looks back to see if he is safe.
CRASH!
"Look out!" yells Elephant. But it is too late. Giraffe goes crashing through the orange grove. All Elephant's oranges fall off the trees.

Parrot sits in a tree,
flapping her wings.
"Why didn't you warn me?"
yells Elephant.
Monkey is stealing the oranges
but Elephant does not see.
He stamps off in a temper.
"That Parrot is too quiet,"
he grumbles.

Soon he meets Lion and Spider.
Just then Alligator arrives.
"Have you heard?" gasps
Alligator. "Parrot's voice
is back. Kangaroo cured it
with lemon and honey."
"Hooray," they all shout.
"Oh no," moans Monkey nearby.
"Now she can tell on me again."
"And again and again,"
screeches chatty Parrot.

Here are some words in the story.

twice	warm
squawks	cross-eyed
screeches	overflowing
voice	flooding
buzz	shelter
trail	cured
tickle	nearby